HAND-ME-DOWN

MAGIC

PERFECT PATCHWORK PURSE

ALSO BY COREY ANN HAYDU

Hand-Me-Down Magic #1:
Stoop Sale Treasure

Hand-Me-Down Magic #2:
Crystal Ball Fortunes

COREY ANN HAYDU

HAND-ME-DOWN
MAGIC

PERFECT PATCHWORK PURSE

illustrated by
LUiSA URiBE

 KATHERINE TEGEN BOOKS

Katherine Tegen Books is an imprint of HarperCollins Publishers.

Hand-Me-Down Magic #3: Perfect Patchwork Purse
Text copyright © 2021 by Corey Ann Haydu
Illustrations copyright © 2021 by Luisa Uribe

Library of Congress Control Number: 2020949385
ISBN 978-0-06-287829-8 — ISBN 978-06-297827-1 (pbk)

Typography by David DeWitt
21 22 23 24 25 PC/LSCH 10 9 8 7 6 5 4 3 2 1
❖
First Edition

To my neighborhood,
which is a little like Alma and Del's,
with its own brand of magic,
bravery, and beauty

ALMA'S HOME,
WHERE SHE WISHES
THERE WERE A LITTLE
MORE MAGIC →

TITI ROSA, EVIE,
AND A LOT OF
LAUGHTER LIVE HERE →

DEL LIVES HERE WITH
HER FAMILY AND AT
LEAST A MILLION
MAGICAL PLANS →

IF YOU'RE LUCKY,
ABUELITA IS
MAKING TOSTONES →
AND GIVING
ADVICE IN HERE

THE CURIOUS
COUSINS
SECONDHAND →
SHOPPE

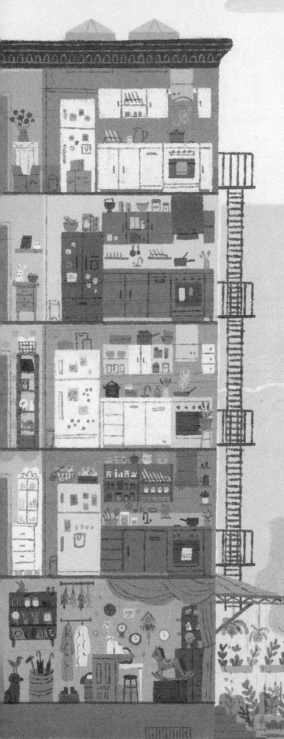

86 ½
TWENTY-THIRD
AVENUE

ABUELITA'S
WILD AND MARVELOUS
BACKYARD GARDEN

Stripes and Flowers and Polka Dots and Plaids

-Alma-

When Cassie came into the Curious Cousins Secondhand Shoppe, Alma could tell she knew exactly what she wanted.

"That," Cassie said. She pointed at the purse that had been hanging in the window all month. It was a patchwork bag, made from at least thirty different fabrics. It was yellow and silver and blue and purple. It had stripes and flowers and polka dots and plaids. Parts of it sparkled. Parts of it shined.

It was beautiful. It was special. It was strange. And it was supposed to be Alma's.

"Oh," Alma said sadly. "Are you sure?"

"Totally sure!" Cassie replied. "I've been saving up for the entire school year to buy something special. And this is it. This is my something special."

Alma nodded. Cassie had talked for months about coming into the store to buy her something special. And Alma had been excited to see what she would pick! But she never imagined Cassie would pick the perfect patchwork purse. Alma wasn't sure if she believed in magic, but that purse looked magical. It looked like maybe, *maybe*, it might be the kind of magic Alma could finally understand.

And Alma didn't know how to say that to Cassie.

"Great pick!" Alma's cousin and best friend, Del, said. "That purse is *really* special."

Alma's littlest cousin, Evie, ran to get the

ladder so she could be the one to climb up to get the purse. Their family cat, Fraidycat, bounded behind her. Fraidycat was always curious, and Evie was always doing something that made her extra curious. Maybe Evie was Fraidycat's something special.

Alma had been thinking the purse was *her* something special. She had been the first person to see the purse. She'd been helping Abuelita go through bags of donations, and the purse had been at the very bottom of one. At first, Alma had thought it was weird. Maybe even ugly. But the longer the purse hung in the window, the more beautiful it became.

Alma loved having the purse in the window. It reminded her that even though she didn't believe in magic the way Del did or the way Abuelita did—which was a whole lot—she believed things were not always what they seemed. She believed that something ordinary could become something special. And she believed that maybe, someday, she'd be the kind of person who could use a magical-looking purse like that.

Alma was thinking all of that, but it sounded too silly to say out loud.

"Maybe you'd like this purse more?" Alma said to Cassie, holding up another beautiful purse that customers were always admiring.

"No, I like this one!" Cassie said. "It's going to be perfect for all the end-of-the-school-year stuff—the parade and the picnic and everything else. I can put my sunglasses in it. And books. And a hat."

Evie came back with the ladder. She was grunting and gasping, pulling the ladder through the store all by herself. Fraidycat swung her tail around, as if she was helping too. "I'll get the purse for you!" Evie said excitedly. Fraidycat meowed in agreement.

"We should ask Abuelita if the purse is really for sale," Alma said. She knew she sounded silly. The purse was hanging in the window! Of course it was for sale!

It was too late, anyway. Evie was scrambling up the ladder, and Cassie was counting out her money, and Del was heading to the back to get Abuelita to ring it up.

Alma kept trying to think of a way to explain why she wanted that purse to stay put. She wanted to be able to say loving that purse made her feel more like the rest of her family at 86 ½ Twenty-Third Avenue. She wanted to tell them all how special she'd felt when she'd been the one who found it. And how when it glittered a certain way, it made her think maybe Abuelita was right, that magic was everywhere.

"¡Qué maravillosa!" Abuelita said when she saw the purse on Cassie's shoulder. And Abuelita was right; the purse was truly marvelous. It was just what Abuelita had said when Alma had first shown it to her. "It really suits you."

Alma thought she might cry.

She wanted Abuelita to tell her that the purse suited *her*. She wanted someone to think *she* should have a sparkly and plaid and flowery and stripy and polka-dotted purse.

Alma wiped away a tear. She swallowed hard. She tried one more time to think of the right words to say to explain to everyone why she was so upset about a purse. But she couldn't find the words to tell them all how it felt to know she had to say goodbye to that little bit of maybe-magic.

How she had hoped it might belong to her someday.

Cassie was happy looking at her brand-new purse. Del and Abuelita and Evie were busy admiring how the purse looked on Cassie.

As usual, Alma was quiet.

She watched as Cassie skipped out of the Curious Cousins Secondhand Shoppe.

"I thought maybe it was meant for me," Alma said. But no one heard.

The Family's Corazón

-Del-

It took three whole days for Del to find out what was making Alma so sad. At first, Del figured it was the end of the school year. When Alma said that wasn't it, Del thought maybe it had to do with missing her old home by the lake. But Alma said no, she was excited for summer in the city this year.

Finally, late one night, Del snuck into Alma's bedroom.

"You have to tell me why you're so sad," Del said. "I can't stop worrying about it."

"Blahgoobaddazzzzzzzzzz," Alma said, because Alma took a really long time to make any sense when someone woke her up in the middle of the night.

"You've been in a bad mood for days," Del said. "Did I do something? Did someone say something mean? Do you have a tummyache? Did you lose something you love?"

"Yes," Alma said. She rubbed her eyes.

"Which one?" Del said.

"I lost something I love," Alma said. "Or I know where it is. But it's not with me anymore."

Del raised her eyebrows. Maybe Alma was still half-asleep. She wasn't making much sense.

"The purse. The one Cassie bought. I wanted it for myself. At least to look at in the store! I just—I guess I miss it."

"That old patchwork purse?" Del said. She didn't think of the purse as something Alma would want. Alma had a navy blue backpack and she didn't like to put pins on it or anything. She had a navy blue notebook and she didn't like to put stickers on it. Alma's room was very neat, and her outfits always matched, and she never wore more than three colors or one pattern at a time.

But Alma's eyes were welling up with tears, so Del was pretty sure she was telling the truth. Alma must really love that patchwork purse.

Luckily, Del was pretty sure she knew how to help!

The next morning, she was happy to find Evie at Abuelita's kitchen counter, eating cremita and planning her Saturday.

"Cancel all your plans!" Del said. "We have a project to do!"

"I love projects. Can I be in charge?" Evie asked, before she even knew what the project was.

"No," Del said. "I'm in charge."

"Can I be second-in-command?" Evie asked.

Del thought about it. "Maybe third," she said.

"Who's second?"

"There is no second-in-command," Del said. She didn't have time to discuss these things with Evie. They had work to do. They needed to gather up all the fabric they could find in all of 86 ½ Twenty-Third Avenue. And then they needed to turn all that fabric into the best patchwork purse anyone had ever seen. Del told Evie to find the prettiest and strangest and funnest fabrics she could. And Del did the same.

When they came back together, they had quite the collection. An old apron of Abuelita's with birds on it, pieces from Evie's polar bear Halloween costume and Del's Wonder Woman costume, fabric samples from Alma's parents, who still hadn't decided on what kind of curtains to put up in their living room, a patch of denim from a jean jacket Del's father was getting rid of, and some scraps of leftover fabric from a dress Titi Rosa was making for their cousin in Puerto Rico who was getting married this summer. Even Fraidycat helped. She dragged her favorite ball of yarn over to the girls and swatted at it. Maybe she wanted them to use it for their project!

"One last thing," Abuelita said when she

found out what the girls were up to. "A bit of our family's corazón."

Del couldn't wait to see what part of her family's heart Abuelita would give them.

She brought out a placemat that Evie sometimes used. It was a map of the world. Abuelita found a pair of scissors and made a few quick cuts. She handed the little bit of placemat-map to Del.

It was a cutout of Puerto Rico.

It wouldn't be easy, but Del was sure they had everything they needed to make the best patchwork purse Alma had ever seen.

A Personalized Purse

-Alma-

"Ta-da!" Del exclaimed Monday morning.

All weekend long, Del and Evie had been up to something. Alma was sure of it. Because Del and Evie kept whispering and disappearing into their rooms and hiding things behind their backs. They even ran up and down the stairs of the building, visiting everyone in the family, and giggling when they left.

And finally here it was, the mysterious project that had been keeping them so busy.

It was in Del's hands. It was very large. It was a hundred different colors. And it was . . . weird.

"It's . . . a . . . purse?" Alma said. It looked sort of like a purse and sort of like a circus tent and

sort of like the garbage the day after someone's
birthday party, when the garbage can was filled
with streamers and bows and wrapping paper.
An explosion of colors and textures.

"A patchwork purse!" Del said.

"A *personalized* patchwork purse!" Evie said. "That means we made it just for you, so it's really special." She looked proud of the word and the purse and herself.

"Oh," Alma said. "Wow. You—you know how to sew?"

"Abuelita helped us," Del said. "So did your mom. Did you know your mom knows how to sew?"

Alma did. Her mother had sewn dresses for her dolls and hems in her pants and, once, even a huge Santa Claus pillow that Alma loved seeing in their living room during the holidays.

Alma had tried to learn how to sew once or twice, but it never went very well. She wondered if Del and Evie were better at it than she had been. Probably.

She looked at the purse. She noticed orange carpet fabric from the carpet they'd gotten rid of upstairs and pink flowery fabric from a pair of pajamas she'd just outgrown. She saw green fabric from the recyclable bags her dad used when he got groceries. She saw birthday wrapping paper and Christmas wrapping paper and maybe even her latest book report? There was something yellow and shiny. Something with black-and-white stripes. Something sparkly and sheer. Something crinkly. Something wrinkly. Something polka-dotted. The straps were ribbons from Titi Rosa's fancy ribbon drawer, and someone—probably Evie—had added three tiny jingle bells to each side.

"Purses are boring," Evie said. "So this is a purse *and* a musical instrument."

Alma wasn't sure she had ever wanted a purse that was also a musical instrument. But it did make a pretty sound.

"We wanted it to be a surprise," Del said.

"We want you to stop being sad," Evie said.

"Well, you did it," Alma said. "I'm not sad anymore!"

And it was true . . . sort of.

Alma was happy that her cousins cared. And she was so busy being confused by all the colors and patterns and ribbons and bells and papers on the purse that she didn't have much room left to be sad.

"What outfit are you going to wear with it?" Del asked.

"It matches everything," Evie said.

"Oh, well, I think maybe I should save it for a special occasion," Alma said. She couldn't quite picture herself wearing it to school. Especially not if Cassie was going to be wearing her new purse to school.

"Like the last day of school!" Del said.

Alma didn't know what to say. She loved her cousins for making this bag for her. But it wasn't magical. It wasn't special the way the purse in the window had been. It didn't make her feel like she was magical and special either.

"Sure," Alma said anyway. "Maybe the last day of school."

But her heart was hoping that somehow the other, magical purse would be hers again someday soon.

4

The Mystery at the
Bottom of the Bag

-Del-

Del had the biggest solo in the end-of-the-year concert, and she'd been practicing it all weekend while she worked on Alma's purse. She was pretty sure she had it down. But she was nervous going into rehearsal anyway. Usually in music class, she stood in the back with Alma. But today everyone with a solo had to stand in the front.

Del was next to Cassie, who had a solo, too, but a much shorter one. The song was about all the beautiful things that grow in the spring

and summer. Del's solo was at the beginning, all about seasons and how great it is when they change. Cassie had a pretty line about roses coming back after the last frost.

Cassie had brought her new patchwork purse to school. All day long she'd been getting compliments on it. Del complimented her, too, but deep down she knew the bag she'd made for Alma was way better.

"I'm so nervous," Del whispered to Cassie.

"Me too," Cassie said. And that's when Del heard it. Cassie had lost her voice!

"Are you okay?" Del asked.

"I went to a baseball game this weekend," Cassie said. "I yelled really loud. I didn't mean to, but everyone else was shouting, so I did too."

"I'm sure it will be fine," Del said. But she wasn't really so sure. Cassie's singing voice was usually really pretty. And she loved singing maybe even more than Del did. But today even her talking voice sounded raspy and wrong. "Do you have a cough drop or something in your purse?"

Cassie shook her head. "All I put in it this morning was a notebook and a couple barrettes." Del wondered what *she* would put in a purse like that if she had one. Maybe she would carry Fraidycat around in it! Now *that* was a good idea!

"I guess it's a good thing I don't have your big solo," Cassie said. "I really wanted to sing that part, but I'm glad you have it now."

"Let's give it a go!" Ms. Henn called out. She sat at the piano and started playing all the familiar notes. Del was up first. Her voice shook. Her knees shook. Even her toes shook! But the notes came out okay, and then it was over. She looked over at Alma.

Her best-friend-cousin was beaming. Del smiled back. She must have really done a good job! It was the biggest smile Alma had had since, well, since Cassie had bought the patchwork purse.

Cassie sang next. Usually, Del loved listening to her sing. But today she didn't sound very good at all. Her voice warbled and broke. Cassie grimaced.

She tried again. It sounded even worse. Scratchy and growly and hoarse. Del wished she could do something to help.

Cassie reached into her patchwork purse. Del was pretty sure her notebook and barrettes wouldn't be able to help. But Cassie's face shifted when her hand hit the bottom. When she pulled her hand back out, Del saw why.

Cassie was holding a teeny-tiny jar. And in the jar was something shiny and amber. Del squinted. There was even teeny-tinier cursive writing on the jar. *Honey*, it said.

"Is this . . . yours?" Cassie asked.

"I don't think anyone brings little jars of honey to school. It's not yours?" Del whispered back. She saw Alma, across the room, straining to see what was happening.

Cassie shook her head. They didn't have more time to talk. They were starting to sing again. While Del was singing, Cassie opened the jar and took a sip. She smiled. Del wished she could taste what was making Cassie smile like that. Cassie took another, bigger, sip of honey. Then she began to sing.

This time, Cassie's voice sounded a little better. A little less hoarse. A little clearer. Actually, kind of pretty.

Del grinned. "Magic," she said.

A Whole Bunch
of Nothing

-Alma-

By the end of the day, Alma didn't want to hear
any more about jars of honey, no matter how cute
and tiny and pretty they were. But she knew Del
couldn't help it. If there was magic to be found,
Del had to find it. And if Del found it, she had to
talk about it.

Sitting at dinner with Abuelita and Titi Rosa
and Evie and all their parents, Alma wished
they could talk about absolutely anything else.
She would like to talk about her favorite book,

or Fraidycat's cutest new trick, or which flavor of ice cream goes best with which other flavor of ice cream. But right now, she wouldn't mind talking about spiders or spinach or even her least favorite book.

"Do you think everything at Curious Cousins Secondhand Shoppe is magical?" Del asked.

Abuelita gave her Abuelita shrug. The Abuelita shrug was one slow shrug followed by one fast shrug and a raise of her eyebrows. Evie tried to imitate it right then, but her slow shrug was too long and her fast shrug was about ten fast shrugs in a row. She squinted instead of raising her eyebrows. It made Alma laugh. Then she remembered to be sad again.

"The jar of honey has to be magical, right?" Del went on. "I mean, Cassie had a sore throat. Then honey appeared and fixed it!"

"Maybe Cassie brought the honey herself," Alma said. "Maybe she just forgot she put it in there. Or her mom packed it for her." She took an extra helping of Abuelita's rice and beans. She didn't know how Abuelita's rice and beans were so especially delicious, but they always were. Even when Alma was feeling grumpy.

"I wonder what kind of magic it is," Del said, not hearing Alma.

"I wonder what kind of magic is in the bag we made you, Alma!" Evie said. She ran to get the bag, and when she came back, she held it in front of Alma. "Try!" she said, opening it up.

Alma stuck her hand in. For a moment she actually believed maybe her purse was magical too. She dug her hand down to the very bottom of the bag. She moved it all around. Maybe there was something in there for her, something she needed just as badly as Cassie needed that honey.

But there was nothing.

Not even a piece of lint.

Alma left the table without bothering to finish her rice and beans or waiting to see what was for dessert.

The Magic That Alma Doesn't Believe In

-Del-

Del found Alma and Fraidycat out on the stoop after dinner. Usually Alma and Del only sat on the stoop in the morning with bagels or in the afternoon while their moms drank tea and chatted about boring grown-up stuff. But the stoop was a good place to go if you were feeling sad, especially if Fraidycat could keep you company. And Del was pretty sure Alma was feeling very sad this night.

"I brought you a cookie," Del said. "Your mom made her special recipe." Del could see that Alma had a lot on her mind. And maybe a cookie wouldn't fix everything. But maybe it would at least help.

"Thanks," Alma said. She took the cookie, and Del sat down next to her. Fraidycat curled up between them.

"Evie said she's going to make a whole batch just for you tomorrow with your mom. She made your mother promise to help her with it."

Del noticed that Alma couldn't help but smile a little. That was the thing about 86 ½ Twenty-Third Avenue. Even when you were feeling gloomy, there was always someone around to make you smile.

"I thought you liked Cassie," Del said when Alma didn't say anything else.

"I do," Alma said.

"And I thought you liked helping people find cool stuff at Curious Cousins."

"I do," Alma said.

"And we made you your own purse," Del said. Now it was Del who felt a little gloomy. She'd thought the purse she'd made would solve everything. She'd worked so hard at it. And still, Alma was sad.

"I know I don't totally believe in it," Alma said, looking out at the playground across the street, "but I still wanted a little magic for myself."

"You want magic?" Del asked. "Even though you don't believe in it?"

Alma gave an Abuelita shrug. "I want everyone to think I'm special, the way you and Evie and Abuelita and now Cassie are all special. And that purse—it made me feel like I'd found a little bit of magic and specialness all by myself."

Del wanted to understand. "Is it like last year when I wanted to be chosen for the big solo for the concert but they chose an older kid instead?"

Alma gave another Abuelita shrug. But she also gave a little smile. "Yep, except this year you got the big solo. Because you're amazing."

"Is it like when Evie thought that princess from England visiting America meant a princess might come by our apartment and she spent a whole weekend learning how to curtsy and deciding what dress was the most royal? And then she found out the princess wouldn't be making a stop at 86 ½ Twenty-Third Avenue?"

Alma smiled again. Del could tell she didn't exactly want to smile, but she couldn't help it. Evie had that effect on people.

"I guess it's a little like that," Alma said.

Del nodded. Alma nodded back.

Del wasn't sure how to make Alma feel better. But she would figure it out. She missed her happy, silly, not-sitting-on-the-stoop-at-night cousin. And it was her job to get her back.

Less Magical by
the Minute

-Alma-

Alma knew everyone wanted her to stop feeling
sorry for herself. So she tried the next morning.
She really, really did. She tried all the way from
her apartment to the front stoop, where she met
Del for their walk to school. She tried the whole
walk to school. And she tried as she walked from
the school's front door to her classroom. But
when she got to her classroom, there was Cassie.

And there was the perfect patchwork purse.

And there was Cassie smiling and telling

everyone about the jar of honey she'd found in it yesterday, and how maybe it was magical. She talked about the color of the honey and how sore her throat was. How mysterious it was that the purse had given her just what she needed. Cassie talked about her magical bag in math and reading and Spanish class. She talked about her magical bag at recess. And she talked about her magical bag at lunch, sitting next to Del. It was where Alma usually sat.

And she wore her perfect patchwork purse over her shoulder the whole time. Alma had never seen someone wear a purse to lunch, but Cassie made it look natural and cool.

Alma tried to change the subject. "I think my Spanish is getting much better from living with Abuelita and Titi Rosa and everyone!" she said. "Mucho mejor!"

But Cassie didn't hear her and kept talking about the honey.

"Mom's taking me to a movie tomorrow after

school. What should we see?" Alma asked. But now Del was talking about the honey too.

"Our little cousin, Evie, has an imaginary friend named Lulubelle. She's a hedgehog. Do you think that's weird?" Alma tried, but no one heard her.

"Del and I have a lot in common!" Cassie said. "We're both a little magical, I guess. Maybe I should work at the Curious Cousins Second-hand Shoppe too!"

Alma's stomach dropped. Her whole body responded to what Cassie said. Her eyes welled up and her fingers shook and her elbows slid off the table. And her slippery elbows made something else happen too. Alma's body responded so strongly to the idea that Cassie might replace her, and that Del probably had more in common with Cassie anyway, that the orange juice Alma was holding spilled everywhere. It dripped off the table. It soaked Cassie's lunch tray. And it got all over Alma's lap.

But most of all, it got on Cassie's purse.

"Oh!" Cassie exclaimed. "Oh no!"

"I'm so sorry!" Alma said, and she really was sorry. She hadn't meant to spill the juice and she hadn't meant to ruin the purse. She was so scared of Cassie taking her place in her family that she had accidentally made a huge, messy mistake.

Cassie looked like she might cry, and Alma thought she might cry too. All her jealousy over this purse was making her do all the wrong things! Cassie was just excited about the purse, and Alma couldn't find a way to be happy for her.

Cassie reached into her purse to see if the juice had soaked all the way through.

When her hand emerged, it wasn't holding a

tiny jar of honey. Instead, Cassie was holding something delicate and white and covered in flowers.

"What's this?" Cassie asked.

Del reached for it. She unfolded it. "A handkerchief?" she said. Alma knew Titi Rosa and Abuelita both had handkerchiefs in their pockets all the time. Nothing this pretty, though.

"What am I supposed to do with it?" Cassie asked. Del turned it this way and that.

"Clean up, I guess?" she said at last. She dabbed at Cassie's purse. And like magic, the orange juice lifted off the purse and onto the handkerchief.

"My turn!" Cassie said. She rubbed and rubbed and soon not a single drop of orange was on the purse. It wasn't even wet.

"Magic," Del said with a grin.

"It really is!" Cassie said, hugging the purse close to her heart.

Alma was relieved she hadn't ruined Cassie's purse. And it was sort of cool seeing something magical happen. And seeing that magical something made Alma a little hopeful that some magic was waiting for her somewhere too.

Alma reached into her pockets, wondering if maybe a magical surprise would appear there. But her pockets were empty.

She felt empty too.

Empty, and less magical by the minute.

Something Secret

-Del-

Del hadn't meant to make such a big deal about the flowery handkerchief, but she couldn't help it. It was light as a feather, and the flowers on it were shiny and sparkly, and somehow it wasn't even dirty from the orange juice spill it had just cleaned. Clearly, it was magical. And Del loved anything magical.

Alma barely spoke after lunch. She didn't sing in music class, and she didn't help come up with ideas for the end-of-the-school-year parade

in art class. She didn't even talk with everyone else on the way home about what to bring to the end-of-the-school-year picnic.

In fact, Del noticed that Alma didn't talk at all.

"It's just a handkerchief," Del said when they reached the playground and Alma sat on the bench instead of running to the swings like she normally would.

"It's magic," Alma said.

"You'll find your own magic," Del said. "Abuelita always says that there's more than enough magic for everyone."

Alma shrugged. Not an Abuelita shrug. Just a sad, sorry, bad-day shrug.

Del still needed to find a way to get her best-friend-cousin back to herself. And she knew just who to ask for advice. Abuelita always had the best advice, especially when it came to things like family and magic. So when they got home, Del went straight to Abuelita's apartment. She

found Abuelita cooking dinner and singing to herself. Del climbed onto a stool and sang along for a minute before telling Abuelita why she had really come.

"Alma thinks she can't be happy without Cassie's purse," Del said. "She thinks she needs it so that she can be magical. And special. And I don't know how to show her that's not true."

Abuelita nodded her head. "Sometimes magic needs a little help," she said. "Alma is just as magical as anyone else, but sometimes magic needs a little push."

Abuelita gave an Abuelita shrug. She also gave an Abuelita wink, which was even better. Abuelita gave great advice, but she never told Del exactly what to do. Del had to figure that out on her own. Or maybe with the help of her littlest cousin.

It took a while to find her—no one had seen Evie since school let out—but finally Del found her hiding in the laundry hamper.

"What are you doing in here?" Del asked.

"Playing hide-and-seek!" Evie said. She always wanted to play hide-and-seek.

"With who?" Del asked.

"Señor Vaca," Evie said matter-of-factly. Señor Vaca was Evie's favorite stuffed animal—a cow wearing a bow tie that Abuelita had gotten her the day she was born. Del didn't have the heart to tell her that Señor Vaca probably wasn't very good at the seeking part of hide-and-seek.

"Can you take a break and help me with something?" Del asked.

Evie leaped right out of the hamper. "Something dangerous?" she asked, excited.

"No, not dangerous."

"Something mysterious?"

"I guess a little," Del said.

"Something secret?" Evie asked. She was getting more and more excited.

"Yes," Del said. "Secret and nice."

"Nice?" Evie asked. Del knew *nice* didn't sound as fun as *dangerous* did to Evie, but she also knew Evie would do anything to make Alma happy.

"We have to make the purse we made for Alma even *more* magical," Del said.

"It's already pretty magical," Evie said.

"Alma doesn't see that yet," Del said. "So we have to show her."

Evie nodded. Del and Evie both knew that sometimes magic was hard to see, especially if you didn't look for it. They got to work.

A Big Shiny Mess

-Alma-

When Alma woke up the next morning, Del and Evie were already in her room, waiting for her to get out of bed.

"Breakfast time already?" Alma asked.

"This isn't about breakfast!" Del said.

"This is about magic!" Evie said.

Alma didn't want to hear anything else about magic. She didn't want to think about magic. She didn't want to hope for magic. She just wanted to pretend she'd never heard of magic.

But that wasn't possible at 86 ½ Twenty-Third Avenue, where her family was certain there was magic in the rosebushes and in Abuelita's empanadas and even in Fraidycat's warm little purr.

"We think something is going on with your purse," Del said. She held the purse out to Alma. Her eyebrows wiggled.

"What do you mean?" Alma asked. The purse looked the same to her. Mismatched and strange and lopsided and not very magical at all.

"It was glowing," Del said.

"And shaking," Evie said. "Magically shaking."

Alma didn't know what her cousins were up to. So she took the purse from Del's hands and reached inside. She tilted the bag, then turned it over.

Out of the bag came a storm of glitter and rhinestones.

"Behold!" Evie proclaimed. She sounded like

the ringleader at the circus they'd gone to a few weeks ago. "Magic!"

It was more glitter than Alma had ever seen at one time, more sparkle than anyone had ever seen, probably.

Evie grinned. Del gasped. But Alma's face fell. There was glitter absolutely *everywhere*. All over her favorite quilt. All over her teddy bear, Oso. All over her homework that was sitting on her bedside table. It was an enormous mess.

"Doesn't it look beautiful?" Del said. "Your purse is even more magical than Cassie's!"

Alma wanted to make Del and Evie happy. She wanted to enjoy the sparkly mess. She wanted to believe her purse was magical. And mostly she wanted to stop feeling sorry for herself.

But sitting in a big storm of glitter, Alma couldn't feel anything but sad.

This wasn't magic, she thought. This was simply more proof that Alma was just boring, unmagical, not-fitting-in Alma. In fact, she was so very, very unmagical that her cousins had to pretend there was magic around her just to make her feel better.

Alma had never felt less magical in her whole life.

You Never Know Where

-Del-

"Let's have breakfast with Abuelita!" Del said after they'd cleaned up as much glitter as they could. Del knew she needed to find magic for Alma, and Abuelita's home was the best place to find it!

All three girls knocked on Abuelita's door. It was locked. It was never locked! When Abuelita came to the door, she was still in pajamas and a robe. Abuelita was never in pajamas and a robe!

"Estoy mal, my girls," Abuelita said, explaining

that she was feeling sick. "I think I have a cold. And a cough. I'd love to have you over for breakfast, but I don't want you to catch anything."

Del and Alma and Evie understood, of course. But Del couldn't help feeling disappointed. Abuelita's apartment was the best place to find magic in all of 86 ½ Twenty-Third Avenue. Probably in the whole city. Maybe even in the whole *world*!

"I know where we can find magic!" Evie said. She ran upstairs to her apartment, and Del and Alma trailed behind. Fraidycat scampered up the stairs too. But even the silly way Fraidycat stumbled up the stairs didn't make Alma smile.

Evie's apartment was filled with flowers that Titi Rosa had just taken in from the garden. Del thought maybe that's where they'd find magic, but Evie went straight for the front hall closet.

"What's in there?" Del asked.

"Not magic," Alma said.

Evie emerged with three hats. One was a sun

hat Titi Rosa used in the garden. One was a gray wool hat Evie's dad wore. And one was a cowboy hat Evie's mom had brought back for Evie from a business trip she took last year.

"Hats?" Alma said, wrinkling her nose. "It's really okay, Evie. I'm okay. We need to get to school. We don't have to—"

"Magicians love hats!" Evie said. "They pull things out of them! We should at least try!"

"Abuelita does say you never know where you're going to find magic," Del said, but even she wasn't too sure about this plan.

"If magicians have magical hats, we probably do too," Evie said, as sure as ever. She reached her hands into each hat. Each time, her face looked hopeful, then surprised to find nothing inside. No bunnies. No scarves. No doves. Nothing magical to make Alma forget about Cassie's purse.

"It's okay," Alma said. "I don't really believe in magic anyway."

"But with the purse—" Del started.

Alma shook her head. "That purse probably wouldn't have been special at all if I'd taken it home," she said. Her voice shook a little. "It's probably only special now because Cassie is special."

Del wasn't ready to give up. She'd cheered Alma up when Alma had broken her arm a few summers ago. She cheered her up at the end of sad movies. She cheered her up when she was missing her old home, on a lake far away from the city. And Alma had cheered Del up when she thought she had a bad luck fortune on her birthday, and when she messed up at her last soccer game, and a hundred other times too. Del knew if they could find even the smallest bit of magic, Alma would be herself again.

On their walk to school, Del looked everywhere for their favorite dog, Oscar. He was so cute, he was surely magical. But when she found him, he was too busy chasing a squirrel to come say hi to them. The sobbing willow tree that looked more magical than anything else on their street was behind a huge truck when they passed it, so they couldn't get a glimpse of its probably magical leaves.

Most days, Del could find magic almost everywhere she looked—in the shape of clouds in the sky or the way a bird was tweeting or even in what the chalkboard outside her mom's favorite coffee shop said.

But today, everywhere Del looked, everything was very, very, very unmagical. Even the chalkboard outside the coffee shop just said Coffee Inside, the most boring, unmagical message it had ever had.

"I'm sorry," Del said when they reached their school's front door.

"I haven't had magic my whole life," Alma said. "There wasn't any magic at the lake. So it's okay that I don't have any here either."

But Del knew it really wasn't okay at all.

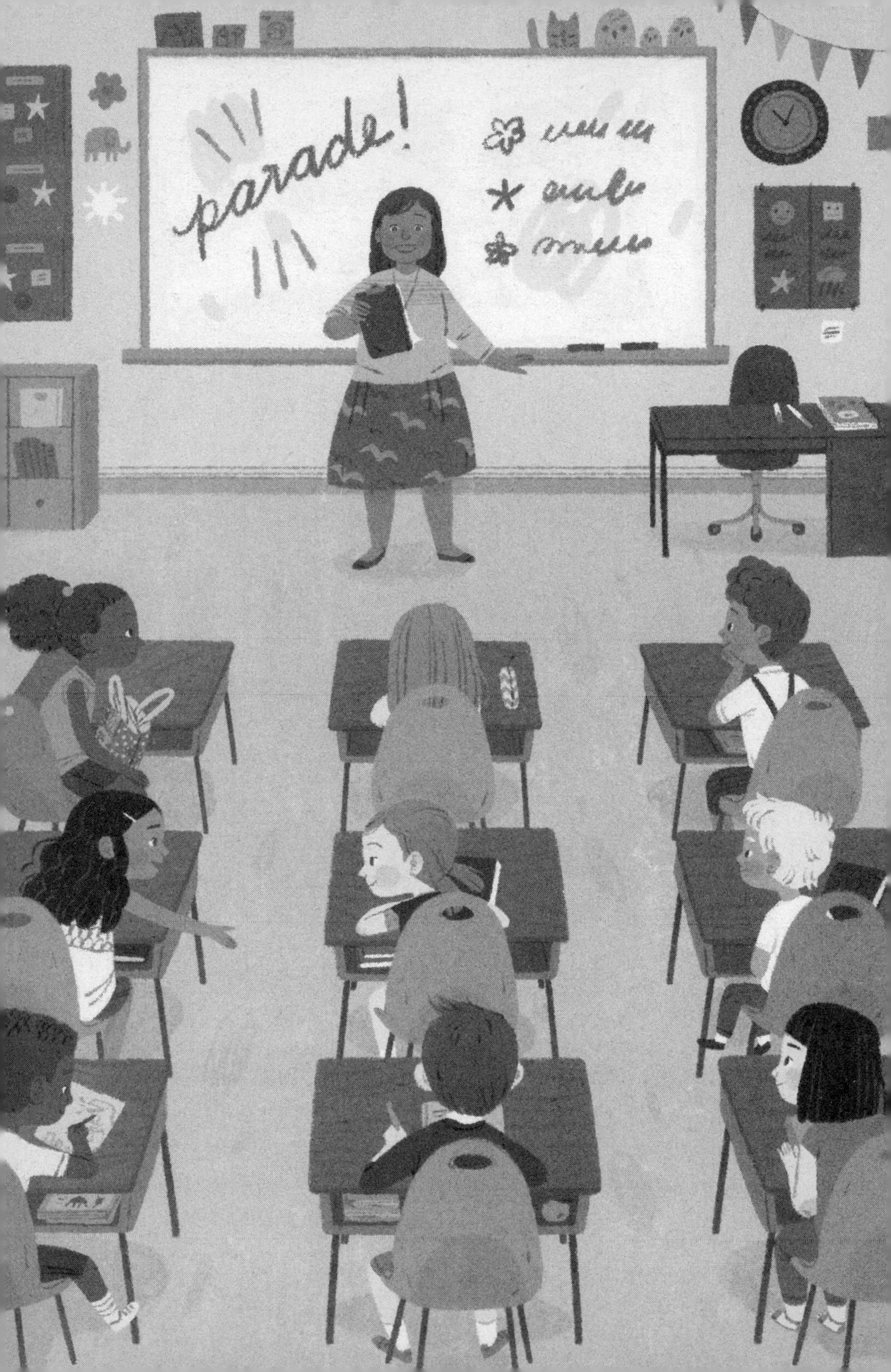
parade!

A Stolen Idea

-Alma-

At school, everyone was getting ready for the end-of-the-school-year events. There was the concert and the picnic and the parade. Alma was especially excited about the parade. Every grade at school got to decorate a float for it, and Del said it was always so much fun.

A few weeks ago, Alma had thought of a million cool ideas for it. They could make it look like a dragon, or like a slice of pizza, or make it look like a beach, with sand and seashells and a big papier-mâché sun. They could all wear bathing suits and maybe they could even use sprinklers so that there could be water too. When she thought of that idea, Alma knew it was the best one. Plus, it would remind her of her old home on the lake. It was truly perfect.

But now she was pretty sure it wasn't a good idea at all.

"We have to decide as a group what we'd like our float to be," their teacher, Ms. Henn, said. "Who has thoughts?"

Alma could tell Del was looking at her, waiting for her to share all her great ideas. Alma wasn't really in the mood. Probably what she'd come up with wasn't so great anyway.

"Can it be purple?" Felix asked. Felix loved purple.

"It has to be more than just purple," Del said. "It needs to be something creative."

"Purple is creative," Felix said.

"Purple's just a color," Del said. "Alma has all kinds of creative ideas."

"Well, we'd love to hear them!" Ms. Henn said.

"I don't know . . . ," Alma said. She wanted to tell them about the dragon and the pizza and the beach. She wanted to say they could even have purple towels or purple bathing suits or, who knows, a purple papier-mâché sun! But she didn't feel very sure of herself. She didn't feel like someone special enough to contribute. Still—Del was nodding at her, and Ms. Henn was smiling, and even Felix and Agatha and June were begging her to tell the class her ideas.

The only person who wasn't looking at her was Cassie. Cassie was looking in her purse, digging around for something.

"Well, I was thinking—" Alma started.

But before she could say another word, Cassie gasped. "Oh my gosh, look!" she said.

Alma didn't want to look.

But everyone else did.

Cassie held up one single, perfect seashell. It was pink and shiny. It was curved and probably sounded like the ocean inside. It was beautiful.

"It's a sign!" Cassie said. "We should decorate the float to look like the beach!"

Alma's heart dropped.

"What a wonderful idea!" Ms. Henn said.

"That's going to be *so cool*!" Felix said.

"You can wear a purple bathing suit, Felix!" Cassie said, just like Alma was going to say.

Everyone in the room was grinning and shouting out beach-float ideas, and complimenting Cassie on her creativity and asking to hold the magical seashell.

"See? The beach is a great idea, Alma," Del said. "I bet you can come up with all kinds of cool other ideas too! You know tons about beaches. It all worked out!"

But Alma shook her head.

Del was right. The beach was a great idea. The best idea. It was absolutely perfect. And no matter what her best-friend-cousin said, Alma knew she'd never come up with a better idea than that one.

Oh!

-Del-

Del had been thinking Alma was being a little silly. What was the big deal, anyway? They were surrounded by magic all the time! What did they need a magical purse for?

But after Cassie found the seashell, Del finally saw how wrong she'd been. The purse had taken Alma's great idea. The purse was making Alma sad. And now it was making Del sad too. She wanted everyone to know how special Alma was. She wanted Alma to feel good about sharing all her great ideas. And most of all, she just wanted everything to go back to the way it had been before the purse.

As the rest of the class made fish out of construction paper and discussed how to get sand onto the float, Del sat at her desk and thought. She understood why trying to make a magical purse just like Cassie's hadn't worked. Abuelita always said magic was one of a kind, just like people.

They needed the perfect patchwork purse, with its special kind of magic. Cassie was very nice. Maybe she would just give it back. But that didn't seem exactly fair. Cassie had saved up for that purse. She'd wanted something special and magical and all her own. Abuelita said that everyone deserves their own special magic, and Del knew that was certainly true for Cassie.

Besides, Del knew what it felt like to work hard for something and be excited when you got it. It's how Del felt about her extra-special, extra-long solo at the extra-special end-of-the-school-year concert. In fact, back when it was announced, Cassie looked pretty disappointed that she wasn't chosen for the big solo because she'd worked hard for it too.

Oh! Del's heart skipped a beat. Her eyes lit up. She covered her mouth with her hands. She knew exactly how to get the purse back. She had something very special. Something that Cassie wanted even more than the magical patchwork purse. And Del knew that abso-lutely nothing was more special than making her best-friend-cousin happy.

Del went up to Ms. Henn. She whispered something in her ear.

"Are you sure?" Ms. Henn asked. Del thought about it for

one more moment. It was hard to give up, but she was sure. She nodded. "If that's what you want, it's okay with me," Ms. Henn said at last. "Why don't you tell her?"

Del practically ran over to Cassie. She pulled her aside. She whispered something in Cassie's ear. Just like Ms. Henn, Cassie said, "Are you sure? The solo is way more important than this silly—"

"Very sure," Del said. "Besides, everyone knows you're the best singer in the grade. Your voice is like magic." When she said it, she knew it was true. Maybe that's what Abuelita meant by everyone having a special magic all their own.

Cassie smiled and blushed. She thought about it. Del wondered if maybe she was wrong, that what she was offering wasn't going to work after all. But before another minute passed, Cassie took her purse off the back of her chair. She took out her three sparkly cat notebooks and her baseball pencil case. She took out her green sunglasses and the book she was reading.

And she handed the purse over to Del.

Del hugged it to her chest.

"Thank you," Del said.

"Thank *you*," Cassie said.

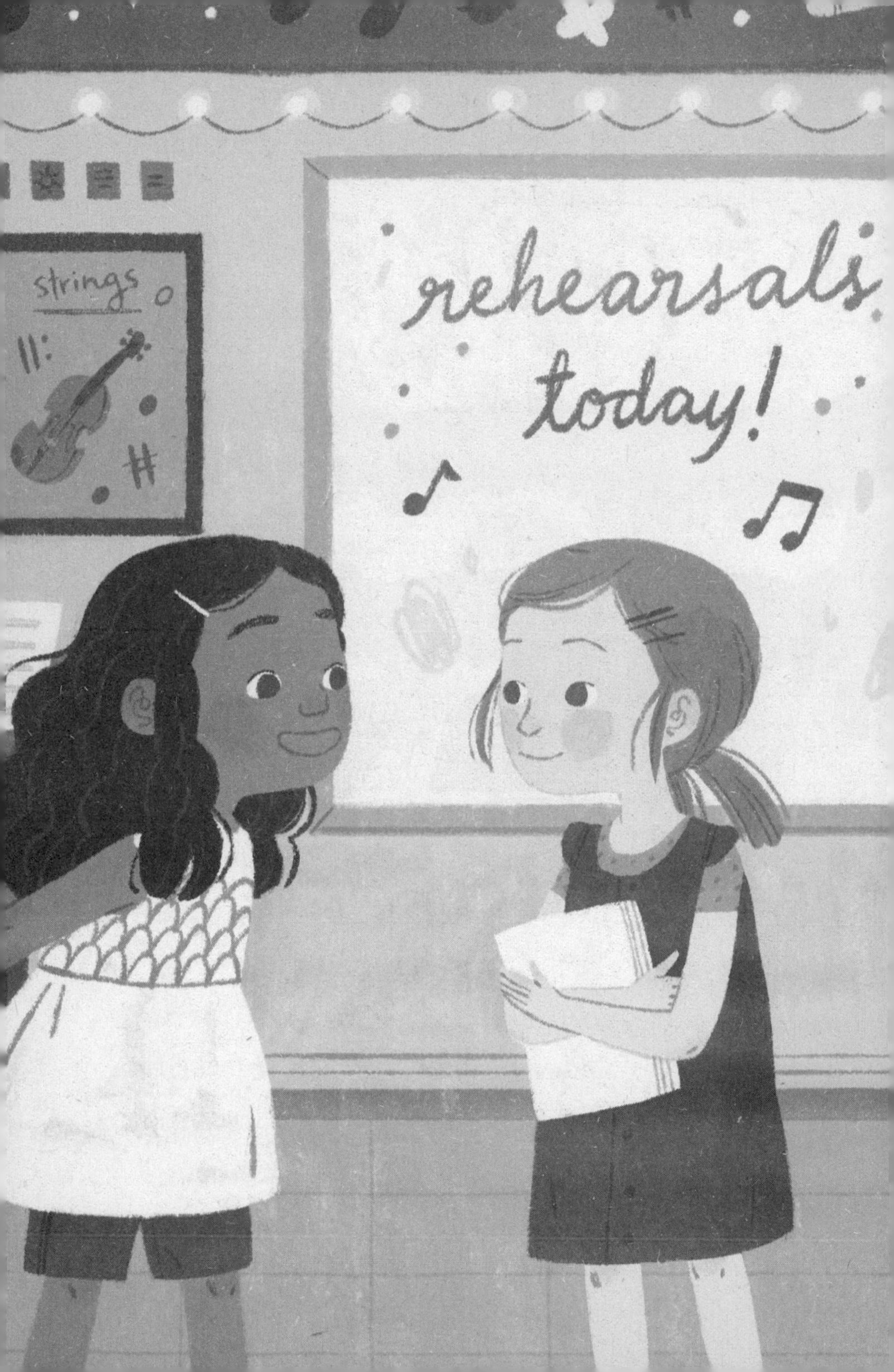
strings
rehearsals today!

Not Borrowed, Not Stolen

-Alma-

Right before the concert rehearsal, Del came up to Alma. Her hands were hidden behind her back. She was smiling so big it made Alma smile, even though Alma had felt like she'd never smile again. Even when she was her saddest, Alma was always happy to have a best-friend-cousin like Del.

"I have something for you," Del said. It's what Del always said when she'd gotten a treat for them to share. Sometimes it was a donut from the shop near their apartment. Sometimes it was a bag of dulce de coco from Abuelita's special drawer of delicious treats, where she stored miniature chocolate bars left over from Halloween and chocolate bunnies from Easter and the special coconut candies that she'd grown up eating. Sometimes it was an extra serving of fries from the cafeteria.

"What is it?" Alma asked. With Del having such a big smile, it must have been something truly delicious and unexpected.

Del brought her hands out from behind her back. Alma gasped. She couldn't believe it. Del was holding the perfect patchwork purse! *Cassie's* perfect patchwork purse!

"She's letting me borrow it?" Alma asked.

"Nope!" Del said.

"You stole it?" Alma asked. She loved the purse, but she already felt bad about spilling juice on it. She didn't want Del to have stolen it!

"No way," Del said.

"So . . . ?"

"So it's yours now," Del said.

"How?" Alma asked. Cassie was nice and everything, but she wouldn't just give up her magical purse, Alma was sure of that.

"We made a trade," Del said.

"What could possibly be as good as a magical purse?" Alma asked.

But before Del had a chance to answer, Ms. Henn clapped her hands together and asked them to get in formation to practice the big song for the concert. Alma went to the back of the room, and Del made her way to the front. Alma was looking forward to hearing her cousin's beautiful voice sing the first verse of the song.

Ms. Henn played the opening few notes on the piano. But instead of Del's voice, it was Cassie's that rang out, singing beautifully about leaves on trees and how green and shiny they are.

At first Alma was confused. But only for a second before she realized what was so valuable that Del was able to trade it for a magical purse. Her solo. Del had given up her special solo so that Alma could have her own little bit of magic.

Alma couldn't believe it.

But then, of course, she could believe it. Del would do anything for her. And Alma would do anything for Del too.

Shake, Shake, Shake

-Del-

"Well, let's see what kind of magic it brings us!" Del said when she and Alma got home. They were sitting on Alma's bed. Evie ran in with Fraidycat a moment later. Evie and Fraidycat always knew when something exciting was happening with Alma and Del, and they always wanted to join in. Evie and Fraidycat both belly flopped onto the bed. A cloud of glitter poufed up as soon as their bodies landed. Fraidycat's black fur was quickly covered in glitter.

"I'm hungry. Do you think the purse will bring us burgers and milk shakes?" Evie asked, trying to wipe glitter off her nose. She wasn't very successful.

"Probably not," Del said. "But we could go to the kitchen and make burgers and milk shakes with Alma's dad if you're hungry."

"No," Evie said. "I'm only hungry for *magical* burgers and shakes." Evie gave her almost-Abuelita shrug. This time it involved a shoulder shimmy and lots of blinking really fast.

"Cassie only found little surprises inside," Alma explained. "Nothing too big. Just small magic."

"Oh," Evie said. "Well, I like big surprises. Like surprise parties! Or surprise trips to Disney World! We should find that kind of purse!"

"Maybe next time," Alma said. Del watched as Alma smiled. It was very easy to love Evie, even when she was silly and ridiculous and jumping up and down on the bed with excitement. "Do you want to reach in first?" Alma asked her littlest cousin.

Evie sat up straight. "Really?" she asked. "Me? Are you sure?"

Alma nodded.

"You're *sure*?" Del asked. She knew how much the purse meant to Alma.

"Very sure," Alma said with a knowing smile. "Cousins do nice things for each other. I learned that today."

Del grinned. She might not have the biggest solo in the concert anymore, but she had the best cousins in the world, and a magical purse.

"Besides," Alma said, "Abuelita always says magic is a good thing to share."

Evie reached her hand into the bag. She waved it around. She took the bag and turned it upside down. She shook it. She shook it even harder. But nothing came out.

"It's broken," Evie said, confused and annoyed. "Why did you get a broken purse?"

"No way," Del said. "Let me try." So Del tried too. She pulled and squeezed and wiggled her fingers around in it. She even tried throwing it in the air. Still, nothing came out.

"Maybe I have to do it, since it's my bag," Alma said.

"That's probably it," Del said. She handed the bag to Alma. Alma reached and wrangled. When that didn't work, she stuck her whole head in the bag. But there was nothing there. Not so much as one magical pebble. It was empty.

"I don't get it," Alma said.

Del didn't understand either. And she was getting very frustrated. Weren't they supposed to be the most magical family on Twenty-Third Avenue? Hadn't she made a good trade for her cousin? Wasn't this supposed to solve everything? What had gone wrong?

"Try again," Del said. And Alma did. But nothing happened. The purse had no magic for the cousins of 86 ½ Twenty-Third Avenue.

And there was only one person who would know what to do about that.

Always, Always

-Alma-

"This purse is broken," Alma said. She was sitting with Del and Evie in Abuelita's kitchen. Abuelita was making Alma's very favorite snack of all time, tostones. They were a little like potato chips but made from plantains and about a million times more delicious, especially when Abuelita made them.

"Broken? Cómo?" Abuelita asked, wondering how a magical purse could break. "Do you need me to sew something? Is there a tear?" She took the purse out of Alma's hands and inspected it. "This does not look broken, mi cielo," she said, using the pet name she used for all her grandchildren. "And anyway, didn't your friend buy this? Isn't this that nice girl's purse?" Abuelita gave her stern-Abuelita look. It was very, very different from an Abuelita shrug. Abuelita's stern look meant she lowered her chin, tilted her head, and made a short *hmm* noise.

"She gave it back," Alma said. It wasn't exactly true, and Alma knew Abuelita could tell.

"I got it back," Del said. "I promise I had her permission."

"But now it's not working. When Cassie used it, it was magical. When I spilled juice on it, she got a magical handkerchief to clean it. And it helped her come up with the best idea for the parade. And then Del traded with her to get it back, but now there's not any magic at all. Cassie must have used all the magic up, and now

there's not any left for me!" Alma's voice shook.
She wanted a bit of magic for herself so badly.

Abuelita smiled. Her stern-Abuelita look was
gone. They all listened to the tostones fry in the
pan. Soon the delicious snack would be sprin-
kled with salt. Alma could practically taste them
already.

Abuelita swayed her body a little to a song on
the radio. She looked out the window. Finally,
she responded.

"You think the magic ran out? You have a lot to learn about magic, mi cielo. That's not how magic works. Not at all. There is always enough magic to go around. You hear me? Always, always. But you can't try to take someone else's magic. You can't try to ruin someone else's magic. You have to believe that there's enough magic for you too. Because there always is. Always, always."

When Abuelita said something twice, it was extra true.

"Always, always?" Evie asked. She looked unsure. Alma felt unsure too. She reached inside the purse again. There was still nothing.

"But there's nothing in here," Alma said. "Nothing, nothing." When she said something twice, it was also extra true.

"Maybe you're not looking with your heart," Abuelita said with an Abuelita shrug. "You're looking very hard with your hands and your eyes. But magic can hide from hands and eyes."

She Abuelita-shrugged again. Evie tried to imitate it again. This time she flapped her hands a little and scrunched up her nose. It wasn't quite right, but it was Evie's, and that made it special, Alma supposed.

"But when Cassie had the bag, she just had to reach inside and there it was. She didn't have to look with her heart or anything. It was there waiting for her, whenever she wanted it," Alma said.

"Oh, Alma," Abuelita said, "what do you need a magic purse for? You have the best kind of magic inside you all the time. The kind that's passed from me to your dad and his siblings to you and your cousins. Hand-me-down magic."

Alma was about to argue with Abuelita, but she took a breath instead. She felt with her heart.

She closed her eyes. She stilled her hands.

And there it was. A little sparkle of feeling

that mixed with the smell of tostones and Abuelita's garden and the sound of Evie starting to tell
a story Alma had heard a million times and the
feeling of Del leaning against her a little.

Hand-me-down magic. Right there in her
heart.

Fair and Square

-Del-

The last day of school was going to be a very busy day. There was the picnic. And the concert. And the parade. But most important, there was one big thing Del and Alma had to do. They had to give Cassie back her purse. Because even though Del had traded for it, it belonged to Cassie. She deserved her special magic. Del and Alma had their own.

The picnic was first. Everyone had to bring a favorite food. Del brought donuts. Alma brought tostones. Felix brought pickles. Cassie brought sandwiches piled high with ham and turkey and two different cheeses. Everyone brought something that they loved or that their whole family loved, and it made the picnic very special and filled with foods Del wanted to eat or had never tried before or had never even heard of before.

Still, Del was pretty sure that her donuts were the best thing there.

"It's time," Del said.

"It's time," Alma agreed.

Del and Alma walked over to Cassie and her pile of sandwiches.

"Hi! Do you two want my famous ham and

turkey and cheese and more cheese sandwiches?"
She looked very proud.

"Sure," said Alma said. "But we have something for you too."

"Something that's yours," Del said.

Alma took the perfect patchwork purse off her shoulder and handed it to Cassie. Del could see it was a little sad for Alma at first, but then she relaxed, and it was just fine. *She must be remembering her hand-me-down magic*, Del thought.

"But this is yours now," Cassie said. "We traded fair and square."

"It wasn't really fair," Del said. "You worked hard to buy this purse."

"And I think it's really meant to be yours anyway," Alma said.

Cassie looked at the purse. She smiled at the way it sparkled and shone and at all the different colors and patterns that somehow looked beautiful together. "Well then, I guess the solo is yours again, Del," Cassie said.

But Del shook her head. She knew they could trade back and have everything be the way it had been before. But she also knew that Cassie would do a great job on that solo. Maybe even a better job than Del. And Del liked singing about roses anyway. It reminded her of Titi Rosa and Abuelita in the garden, tending to their flowers and gossiping about all kinds of things that Del tried to keep up with. "That's okay," Del said. "I think you do the solo really well. I'll keep the part about roses. It's pretty."

"Wow," Cassie said. "You're sure?" Del nodded. Alma nodded too.

"I already have a bag," Alma said. It was her turn to surprise Del. She had brought the purse that Del and Evie had made to the last day of school! She put it over her shoulder. Del thought it looked just perfect on her.

Everyone's Jealous

-Alma-

Cassie sang beautifully at the concert. So did Del. Alma loved listening to them both.

At the parade, Alma, Del, and Cassie all stood together. They were all wearing polka-dotted bathing suits and sun hats and flip-flops. It reminded Alma a little bit of her old home by the lake. But it also reminded her of everything she loved about living right here.

"I have to tell you something," Alma said to Cassie. They were waving their hands at the

moms and dads and grandparents and siblings and friends and families who came to watch the end-of-the-school-year parade go down Twenty-Third Avenue.

"You want the purse back?" Cassie said. She looked worried. Alma had loved that purse a lot, but Cassie might love it even more.

"No," Alma said. "That purse is yours; don't worry. I just have to tell you I'm sorry. I was so jealous of you having the beautiful, magical purse that I couldn't think straight! I wasn't very nice about it."

"You're jealous of this purse?" Cassie asked. Her eyes were wide. "But I'm jealous of *your* purse!" She pointed to Alma's shoulder, where the purse Del and Evie made still hung.

"You're jealous of *this*?" Alma asked. She started to laugh. She couldn't imagine anyone being jealous of her strange, messy, totally bizarre handmade purse.

"Yes!" Cassie said. "I can't believe your cousins made that for you! That's so cool. My cousins live far away. I miss them so much. We have the best time together when we see each other." Cassie pointed out at the crowd. There were so many people cheering for Del and Alma. Evie and Abuelita and their parents, of course. But also Titi Rosa and Uncle Andy and their other cousins and titis and tíos and uncles and aunts who lived nearby. They had all shown up to have fun at the parade and celebrate with Alma and Del. "I wish my whole family lived nearby, like yours," Cassie said.

Alma waved at her family. She waved at Cassie's mom and dad and little brother too. They were clapping and beaming and Cassie's mom was holding a unicorn-shaped balloon that Alma bet was for Cassie.

"Why don't you come have dinner with us on Sunday?" Alma suggested. "We have big family dinners every Sunday. And everyone's invited.

The more the merrier. You can borrow our cousins whenever you miss yours."

"Really?" Cassie asked.

"Absolutely!" Alma answered. "I know what it's like to miss your cousins. I used to miss mine all the time before I moved here."

"I'd love to come over for dinner," Cassie said. "It sounds pretty magical."

All You Need ... and Maybe a Little More

-Del-

Alma insisted that Abuelita make her famous empanadas for Cassie. Alma also made her mother's famous cookies. Del helped with the rice and beans. Evie poured everyone their drinks and did a little welcome-to-dinner dance when Cassie arrived.

But before they sat down to dinner, all four girls went up to Alma's room. Cassie had to tell them about the magical things her purse had done since the parade. She'd found a mysterious coin when she wanted to buy a milk shake and was short on money. And she'd found a magical pencil when hers broke while she was writing a very special poem about magic and family and friends. And best of all, she'd found a magical stamp that was going to help her send a letter to her favorite cousin.

"I still think *this* bag is magical too," Evie said. She was playing with the jingle bells on Alma's purse. She had added another twelve to the handles, because she didn't think it was quite musical enough yet.

"It doesn't need to be magical," Alma said. "You two made it for me, and that makes it very special."

"I think it's really cool-looking," Cassie said. "Plus, everything on it has meaning. It's all little pieces of your family."

"That's true," Alma said.

"But I don't want it just to be special," Evie said. "I want it to be magical."

"We have more than enough magic," Del said. And she mostly believed it.

But Evie wasn't going to give up. She reached her hands into the bag. She waved them around. She explored every corner of that purse.

She almost gave up.

But then her eyes lit up.

"Oh!" she said. "There's something in here!"

Del laughed. "Whatever you say, Evie," she said, and rolled her eyes. "Evie likes to mess around."

"Remember, Abuelita said some magic is just living inside of us," Alma said. "And that's all we really need."

"Well, maybe that's all *you* need," Evie said, "but we got something else too." She pulled her hand out of the bag. And held it out for the girls to see.

There in her hand were four thin silver rings. They almost looked like key rings. They weren't sparkly and they didn't have rhinestones and they weren't fancy. They didn't *look* magical, exactly. But when the girls each took one, they fit their fingers perfectly.

They held their hands up, admiring their little reminder that there was always enough magic—and friendship—to go around. Always, always.

Acknowledgments

As always, there are many hands and hearts and minds that go into the making of this book, and I am beyond grateful for each one.

A huge thank-you to the wondrous Luisa Uribe for her continually magical illustrations that bring these books to life.

Thank you to Mabel Hsu for all the brainstorming sessions, your belief in these books, and the way you treat every sentence, every character, and every story of mine with such care.

Thank you to Victoria Marini for all the big and small ways you help me tell stories.

Thank you to Katherine Tegen for your continued support and the lovely home you've given me and my stories. And thank you to the entire

Katherine Tegen Books team, especially David DeWitt, Tanu Srivastava, Amy Ryan, Alexandra Rakaczki, Maya Myers, Allison C. Brown, Emma Meyer, Sam Benson, and Robert Imfeld.

Alma and Del uncover a
magical mystery in:

HAND-ME-DOWN
MAGIC

MYSTERIOUS TEA SET

Read on for a sneak peek!

Better Than a Gnome

-Del-

On Saturday, the Curious Cousins Secondhand Shoppe was so busy that Del, Alma, and Evie could hardly take a breath. Alma was in charge of making change when a customer paid with cash. She was getting very good at math. Evie was in charge of greeting customers. She did it so loudly that Del either cringed or laughed every time a new person came through the door. Del had the hardest job. It was also the best job. She was in charge of asking customers if they needed any help, and then finding all kinds of strange items when they did. One customer was looking for a cuckoo clock, but she cared very much about what sort of cuckoo noise the clock made. So Del spent part of the morning helping her test the cuckoos. Another customer wanted to know if they had any hats. Of course the Curious Cousins Secondhand Shoppe had a great many hats, so Del searched high and low through every last one. Right before lunch, a man came in looking for a tea set.

"I think we have a few," Abuelita said, darting her eyes this way and that. "Del, go look for some tea sets for our customer, okay?"

"Tea sets coming right up!" Del said. She knew there was a pink tea set on the shelf by a box of old postcards and a green tea set with some broken parts over by the rocking horse. Del walked the aisles looking for more hidden tea sets. There weren't any by the collection of fancy coats and there weren't any in the furniture section either.

Del knelt to the ground in the jewelry section. It was one of her favorite places to spend time—with glittering stones and heavy chains and unmatched earrings and elaborate broaches featuring every imaginable animal and flower.

Del moved a few jewelry boxes aside. Sometimes the shelves got so crowded that important things got pushed to the back. When she moved the heaviest, fanciest jewelry box aside, she found it. A very beautiful tea set. This, she was sure, would be the one the man picked. It looked delicate and sweet, with green and blue designs on it. She was a little sad, actually, that she'd have to say goodbye to this tea set only moments after discovering it.

She brought all the tea sets to the front of the store where the man was enjoying some of Abuelita's homemade gofio. He poured the sugary-sweet powdered candy right into his mouth, and a little bit of it dusted his face.

"I found three tea sets," Del said, placing each

one gingerly in front of the man.

"Bien hecho, Del," Abuelita said. She was always complimenting Del on her object-finding abilities. There was never a disappointed customer at Curious Cousins.

The man and his powdery gofio-fingers picked up pieces of each tea set. And to Del's delight, he shook his head when he picked up the beautiful blue-and-green teapot of Del's favorite set. "My kids really prefer pink," he said. "I'll take the pink one."

Del thought the pink one was sort of boring compared to the blue-and-green one, but she happily carried it to the counter for him anyway. She smiled at Alma, whose face was all scrunched up as she carefully counted out thirty-seven cents of change for a woman buying a bouquet of fake flowers.

"BIENVENIDOS!" Evie said way too loudly, welcoming a family of four who had just walked through the door. "Everything in the store is ten percent off today, so you should get way more than you planned, okay? We have a very nice collection of garden gnomes today. And there's even a chandelier in the back! Want me to show you???"

"Oh, um, we're okay!" one of the new customers said, clearly flustered by Evie's excitement. "We're not really looking for gnomes. Or a chandelier."

Del and Alma exchanged a glance. No matter how many times Abuelita told Evie what to say to customers—exactly what to say to them— Evie always found a way to make it her own.

"Gnomes, huh?" the man with the pink tea set said before handing his money over to Alma. "Maybe I'd be interested in some gnomes. I'll leave this here and he right back, okay?"

"No problem," Alma said. She and Del were having trouble holding in their laughter. Evie was absolutely beaming.

"I would love to show you the gnomes!" Evie

said, bouncing up and down a little. "There are big ones and little ones and a few in-between ones, too, but big or little is probably better, don't you think?"

"1 suppose so," the man said, following now-galloping Evie to the gnome section of the store.

Finally Del and Alma could collapse into giggles. "She's going to sell every gnome in the store by the end of the day," Del said.

"And a chandelier!" Alma exclaimed. She looked at the tea set the man had set down. "This is pretty."

"Don't worry, he didn't choose the really cool tea set," Del said. "I'll show you after he leaves, okay?"